This version has been specially adapted for developing readers in conjunction with a Reading Consultant.

Special thanks to Sarah Levison

ORCHARD BOOKS

This story first published in Great Britain as
'Poppy Muddlepup's Daring Rescue' in 2014 by Orchard Books
This Early Reader edition published in 2018 by The Watts Publishing Group

1 3 5 7 9 10 8 6 4 2

A CIP catalogue record for this book is available from the British Library.

ISBN 978 1 40834 590 0

Printed in China

MIX
Paper from
responsible sources
FSC® C104740
www.fsc.org

The paper and board used in this book are made from wood from
responsible sources

Orchard Books
An imprint of Hachette Children's Group
Part of The Watts Publishing Group Limited
Carmelite House, 50 Victoria Embankment, London EC4Y 0DZ

An Hachette UK Company
www.hachette.co.uk
www.hachettechildrens.co.uk

Poppy Muddlepup

Daisy Meadows

ORCHARD

www.magicanimalfriends.co.uk

Contents

PART ONE
A Rainbow Feather

CHAPTER ONE

To Friendship Forest!

It was a snowy day and Jess Hart and her best friend Lily Forester were helping out at the Helping Paw Wildlife Hospital.

Suddenly, the girls heard a soft miaowing.

"Look," said Lily, pointing outside. "It's Goldie!"

Goldie was a magical cat who lived in Friendship Forest, a secret world full of talking animals! Lily and Jess had been on four adventures there. Each time, the girls had stopped a nasty witch called Grizelda from taking over the forest.

The girls followed Goldie
towards the old oak tree
that stood in the middle of a
meadow. Smiling, they said
the magical words together …
"Friendship Forest!"

A door appeared in the trunk.
The girls went through it. They
were back in Friendship Forest!

"Oh, Goldie, it's so lovely to
be here!" cried Lily, smiling at
their animal friend.

Goldie explained that she
would like to visit Barney,

a dog friend who lived in the human world. It was his birthday. She asked if the girls could keep an eye on things in Friendship Forest whilst she was away.

"Of course!" Lily and Jess agreed straightaway.

The girls spotted two friendly puppies bounding around. They both had very waggy tails.

"I'm Poppy Muddlepup," said one. "This is my twin brother, Patch."

Poppy and Patch took the girls to visit their home, Garden Grove.

"Our plants are magical," Poppy explained. "We use them in potions to make all the poorly animals feel better."

Suddenly, Grizelda appeared.

"I need these magical plants for a potion!" she shrieked.

CHAPTER TWO

A Horrible Spell

Patch jumped up to stop
Grizelda. The witch cast a spell,
and Patch fell into a deep sleep!

"You've got until sunset," she
snarled. "Give the plants to me,
or he will never wake up."

Then she disappeared in an
explosion of sparks.

Jess, Lily and the Muddlepups
tried everything to wake Patch,
but nothing worked!

"I wish Goldie was here!"
Jess frowned. They needed
their magical friend.

"Mrs Taptree might be able
to help," said Poppy. "She runs
an amazing library!"

So Poppy, Lily and Jess
set off. Soon they reached
the hollowed-out trunk of
a chestnut tree. Inside, they
could hear the tap-tap-tap of
a woodpecker.

From inside the tree, a voice
squawked, "Come in! Books
for all in my library!"

The girls and Poppy stepped into the tree hole. It was much bigger than it looked from the outside. The room was packed with books. Mrs Taptree the woodpecker fluttered down from the top shelf.

Poppy explained what had happened to Patch.

"Dear me," said Mrs Taptree.

"Let's look in my books for an answer!"

The girls searched the shelves. Before long, Lily had found a book on magic potions.

Lily flicked through the book, then cried, "I've found a recipe for a Rise and Shine potion!"

Jess read over Lily's shoulder.
"It says, 'Guaranteed to wake
sleepers from even the deepest
slumber'."

Lily turned to Poppy. "So
now all we have to do is find
the right ingredients …"

CHAPTER THREE

A Tiny Friend

Lily read out the recipe. "We need a rainbow feather, some jewel water, and ... Oh! I can't read the last thing. It's smudged!"

"Let's find the first two," Jess suggested. "Maybe then we can work out the missing one."

Poppy had been thinking hard. "A hummingbird has tiny feathers in all the colours of the rainbow …" she began.

Mrs Taptree nodded. "Look for crimson bell flowers and you'll find a hummingbird!" she said.

Poppy darted to the door.

"I'll soon sniff out the flowers!" she cried.

The girls thanked Mrs Taptree and hurried off after the little puppy.

Before too long Poppy found the crimson bell flowers. And there was a tiny, brightly coloured bird!

The beautiful bird hid beneath the flowers' broad leaves.

"Please come out," Poppy said gently. "We really need your help!"

The hummingbird peeped out. "Hello," she said shyly.

Lily explained about the potion and the first ingredient.

"I'll gladly give you a feather," trilled the tiny bird. She fluttered her wings and a magical rainbow feather fell on to Lily's hand.

"Thank you!" said Jess.

"Hooray!" Poppy yapped. "We're going to save Patch!"

The three friends set off back through the forest together, determined to save Patch and Garden Grove!

PART TWO
Jewel Water

CHAPTER FOUR

A Mysterious Girl

Lily and Jess were looking for
jewel water when they bumped
into a friendly-looking girl.
They explained what they
were looking for and why.

"My name's Gretchen," said
the girl. "I know where you
can find the water! Follow me."

Jess and Lily were thrilled. They were going to have everything they needed to break Grizelda's spell!

Gretchen led them to a circle of bushes. "You'll find what you need in there," she smiled. The girls went into the centre of the bushes.

But then the friends realised Gretchen was chanting!

"Branches, twist in thorny curls. Make a cage for nasty girls!"

At once, the bush sprouted
hundreds of sharp thorns.
Suddenly Jess, Lily and Poppy
were surrounded by a thick,
prickly cage.

"We're trapped!" cried Lily.

Gretchen's pretty face appeared above the spiky cage. Then, to the girls' horror, her hair turned green, and the pretty dress became a swirling black cloak.

"It's Grizelda!" cried Lily.

"Gretchen was the witch in disguise!"

Grizelda's cackle echoed round the forest. "You fools! You won't find the jewel water, and you'll never find the Sunrise Berries!

She snapped her fingers and disappeared.

Jess and Lily turned to comfort Poppy. The little puppy's eyes were brimming with tears. "We can't save Patch," she whimpered, "and we're trapped here!"

Lily hugged her. "Don't worry, Poppy," she said. "We'll beat Grizelda!"

"There is one good thing," Jess realised. "Grizelda's told us that Sunrise Berries are the third ingredient!"

Lily nodded. "We just need to get out of this cage, then we can carry on searching!"

CHAPTER FIVE

Mice Mates!

"Ssh," said Poppy. "I can hear squeaking ..."

Lily peered beneath the branches. "It's Molly Twinkletail and her family," she cried.

Jess rushed to the gap and shouted, "Molly! Help us! We're trapped!"

The mouse family set to work, using their sharp teeth to gnaw at the branches. Soon they'd made a gap big enough for Poppy, Lily and Jess to squeeze through.

"Hooray!" cheered the Twinkletails.

The girls and Poppy carried on searching for jewel water.

Before too long Lily spotted a silvery spring. In the sparkling stream were lots of brightly coloured jewels.

"Jewel water," cried Jess, leaning over her shoulder.

"It's the second ingredient!" Lily exclaimed. "But how on earth will we carry the precious water …?"

Poppy's tail wagged as she pulled out a bunch of bottle-shaped blue flowers from her bag. "Bottle blooms. They never spill a drop!" she explained.

The girls carefully poured the shimmering water into the flowers and then tucked the bottle blooms safely into their pockets.

"Now to find the Sunrise Berries," said Jess.

"The Treasure Tree is the tallest tree in Friendship Forest, right?" Lily said thoughtfully. "So, anything growing right at the top of the tree would be the first to see the sunrise. Perhaps that's where we'll find the berries!"

Jess gave a whoop of delight. "You must be right," she cried. "Let's go and search the Treasure Tree!"

CHAPTER SIX

The Treasure Tree

The Treasure Tree was so big that it seemed to fill the whole sky! Long vines dangled around the trunk. Lily picked up Poppy and carefully the three friends started to climb the tree.

"Oh, there's Woody Flufftail the squirrel!" cried Poppy.

The friends
climbed right to
the top of the
tree. But they
couldn't see any
Sunrise Berries.

Jess looked
out past the
forest's edge. She
spotted a tall,

forbidding tower. "That must be Grizelda's home," she said, frowning. "What if the Sunrise Berries grow high up on the tower?"

Back on the ground, poor Poppy's ears drooped. "We'll never save Patch," she sobbed. "Not if the berries are at the top of the witch's tower. No one would dare to go there."

"We dare," said Jess, bravely.

"That's right," said Lily. "We're going to get those berries, whatever it takes!"

PART THREE

Sunrise Berries

CHAPTER SEVEN

To the Tower

The three friends crossed to the far side of the forest. They were close to Grizelda's stone tower, but there was a huge lake to cross first!

Luckily, a family of friendly frogs rowed the friends across the dark water on giant lily pads.

"I wish we had our jackets and mittens back," Lily said with a shiver.

Poppy pulled out three red flowers from her bag. "These will help," she smiled.

Lily and Jess each tucked a flower behind their ears and felt a wonderful warmth surge through them. "Wow!" said Lily. "Your flowers really are magical, Poppy!"

The friends made their way to the tower. The walls were black and crumbling.

Jess pointed. A black vine
had wound its way around the
very top of the tower. Growing
on it was something sparkling
and orange. "Sunrise Berries!"
said Jess, delightedly.

The friends
managed to get
into the tower by
climbing through
an open window.
"Come on," said
Jess, leading the
way up the
dark, dusty
stairs.

Poppy's ears pricked up. "Grizelda's coming!" she whispered.

"Oh, no," said Lily. "Hide!"

Jess spotted a door. She wrenched it open and saw it was a cupboard, full of old cauldrons. Jess, Lily and Poppy darted inside, shutting the door softly behind them.

Moments later, Grizelda climbed down the stairs.

"It'll soon be sunset!" she cackled. "The magic plants will be mine – all of them!"

As Grizelda stomped past, dust billowed around the girls and Poppy.

"Aaah ... aah ..." Oh, no! Poppy was going to sneeze! "*Fwooff!*"

"Who's that?" Grizelda snapped. "Who's there?"

"Quick!" whispered Lily. "Let's hide in one of these big cauldrons."

Grizelda yanked the cupboard door open ...

8CHAPTER EIGHT

The Black Vine

The girls and Poppy stayed as still as they could inside the big cauldron.

Grizelda grunted and slammed the cupboard shut.

"Phew!" Jess said. "Come on – let's get those berries and get out of here!"

They ran to the vine and
Jess reached out to grab
a handful of the berries.
Immediately, jagged shards of
ice appeared on them.

"Oh, no!" cried Jess.
"Grizelda must have put a spell
on the berries!"

"The winter warmers
will melt the ice,"
yapped
Poppy.
They
each held

their winter warmer flowers against the ice. The ice melted and the girls were able to grab handfuls of the berries.

Jess looked up at the sky. "It's almost sunset," she said. "How will we get back to the Muddlepups' den in time?"

"Oh, no!" wailed Poppy. "We're going to be too late to save poor Patch!"

"Listen!" said Lily. "I can hear something." The girls looked around and, to their astonishment, saw a hot air balloon floating towards them. It was pulled by Captain Ace, and in the balloon's basket was Goldie!

"I heard what happened and I guessed you'd be here!" Goldie called. "Now, quick – get into the basket!"

When they were all aboard, Ace flew them over the forest. But it was a race against time.

"The sun has almost set!" cried Lily. "Quick!"

Ace lowered the balloon over the Muddlepaws' den and everyone climbed down the ladder and rushed into the den.

Patch was still fast asleep in his nest of blankets.

The girls started to make the potion for Patch. Jess emptied the jewel water into a bowl, then Lily dropped in the berries and added the hummingbird feather.

There was a fizzing sound as the ingredients dissolved into a swirling orange mixture.

Lily took a spoon and carefully dripped the potion into Patch's mouth.

CHAPTER NINE

Goodbye, Animal Friends!

Patch's nose twitched. Then he opened his eyes!

Jess and Lily felt as if they would explode with relief. But then, just as the sun set, Jess saw an orb of light floating down towards the Muddlepups' den.

Just then, out bounded Patch, looking as bouncy as ever!

Grizelda gasped. "How did this happen?" she shrieked. "You couldn't have made the potion in time! How did the puppy do it?"

Lily's face lit up. "Let's tell her that the Muddlepups are magical," she whispered to Jess.

Jess nodded. "Patch broke your spell," she called. "All the Muddlepups are magic!"

"Including me!" Poppy shouted. She blew on a handful

of purple puffball flowers, releasing bright pink smoke.

"Run, Grizelda!" Lily called. "Poppy just did a spell that makes witches disappear!"

Grizelda shrieked and vanished in a shower of sparks.

Everyone burst into loud cheers. "Hooray!"

A little while later, it was time for Jess and Lily to say goodbye. There were lots of hugs for everyone.

"Bye, Goldie!" cried the girls. Lily opened the door in the Friendship Tree and the two of them stepped into the shimmering golden light.

The girls found themselves back in Brightley Meadow. Snow was falling softly all around them. The girls knew that no time would have passed in the human world while they were in Friendship Forest.

The best friends raced
back to Lily's house and Mrs
Hart made them mugs of hot
chocolate.

Lily and Jess shared a happy
smile. They couldn't wait
for their next adventure in
Friendship Forest!

The End

There's lots of fun for everyone at
www.magicanimalfriends.com

Play games and explore the secret world of
Friendship Forest, where animals can talk!

Join the
Magic Animal Friends Club!

Special competitions

Exclusive content

All the latest Magic Animal Friends news!

To join the Club, simply go to

www.magicanimalfriends.com/join-our-club/